Falling For The Alpha

Van Cole

Published by Van Cole, 2023.

.

FALLING FOR THE ALPHA

First edition. June 2, 2023.

Copyright © 2023 Van Cole.

ISBN: 979-8223529491

Written by Van Cole.

Table of Contents

Falling For The Alpha
Gay First Time MPREG Romance

By: Van Cole

Foreword

Jake Frost was a tearaway once—spending his days committing petty crimes and living up to all those terrible shifter stereotypes that bigoted humans have. A stint in the military had him straightened out, but now he spends his days looking for a job that doesn't want to be found, and his nights running from ugly memories of desert heat and relentless gunfire.

By contrast, Mikhail Debrov has always been on the right side of the law. A police officer and straight-edge single parent, Mikhail has long since suffered with guilt for the passing of his ex-wife. Their relationship was always stilted, and though they stayed together for their son, they never really had the kind of connection that Mikhail now craves.

Years ago, their paths might have crossed in very different circumstances but these days, Jake is a new man, and Mikhail is about to realize that he has some changes of his own to make. Especially when an unforeseen development blindsides them both. Can Jake settle down from the promiscuous lifestyle that numbs his pains, and learn to let family protect him instead? Can Mikhail come to terms with a sexuality he never thought he'd possess? Or will the urban maze let them both stumble away and lose each other forever?

Table of Contents

Falling For The Alpha

Chapter One

Jake

He woke with a start, breath startlingly sharp and cold in his lungs where he had expected to breathe the hot desert air. Here in his chilly apartment, there was no red dust smeared on his forehead and no constant cracks of gunfire outside—just the occasional burst of it when street violence strayed too close to his doorstep. All the same, he was sweating as heavily as if he'd woken up in the desert. As if he was still wearing army fatigues instead of a thin white sheet that clung to his chest and shivered along with the rest of his skin.

It had been six months now since Jake had come home. He had gotten perfectly used to walking with a prosthetic lower leg now, but regrettably it still made sure that he was no longer considered fit for service. An honorable discharge, which frankly didn't feel so honorable at all. His brothers-in-arms were still out there fighting. By the luck of the draw, they were the ones who'd picked shrapnel out of their uniforms and moved on with their military careers. He was all the way back here, in a place he was supposed to think of as home.

It was strange, really, to feel that sense of belonging with the army. Jake had only originally enlisted as an alternative to serving time. Officially, of course, that wasn't the case; the army refused people who were only signing up to skip out jail. That was understandable. On the down-low, however, a sympathetic higher-up with the cops had insinuated that joining the military would do him good. That he might be willing to drop the numerous petty charges against Jake if only he knew that Jake was trying to improve his life—was trying to do something good for himself and for his country.

In the end, that piece of advice had turned out to be the best he had ever been given. The army had straightened him out—or at least, it had straightened his behavior. It was a debt that he felt he had not been given enough time to repay before his injury.

But his moral objection to being discharged was not his only problem. The conviction he avoided by signing up would not have been his first. Jake had started out as a real problem kid—the kind who would have struggled for employment had he ever tried to find it. Now that he was out of the army and had his better head screwed on, he really did want to find work, and his past was still coming back to haunt him.

Veterans had a hard time finding jobs in any case—and God help him whenever an interviewer found out that Jake was a shifter. It was practically a recipe for permanent unemployment. A death sentence in the form of starvation. Not only that, but rent was so high that it was almost criminal. If he didn't find something soon, he'd be shit out of luck, and forced to live on the streets. Perhaps forced to return to his own scavenging ways just to survive.

Either that or he'd leave the city altogether, and live in his other form on a permanent basis. He didn't think he'd miss this form so much. He could vaguely see his reflection in the grubby apartment window—the room small enough that his bed was pressed right up against the window, and practically filled the entire room. He looked like death. He always did after waking up from nightmares of the war, but he knew he hadn't really looked healthy in a long time. He was gaunt, and his sharp cheekbones cut such a hard line on his face that it was obvious how long it had been since his last meal. His eyes were dark. No prizes for guessing why that was.

He swung his legs out of bed, the toes of his remaining foot hitting the wall on the other side, and ran his hands through his hair.

It was 4 a.m. Last night it had been 5:30 a.m. The night before that, 2:55 a.m.

He already knew from experience that there was absolutely no point trying to get back to sleep. Instead, he strapped on his prosthetic foot tight around what remained of his knee and stood up to splash water on his face, picking up his phone from the bedside table as he passed it.

Out in the second room, combining a kitchen with a tiny seating area, he slumped down into the chair and opened up Grindr.

It was the dead part of the night, so he doubted anybody decent would be awake. In fact, it had been a while since he'd stumbled across anybody suitable for a hookup at all. Before long, his promiscuous heart would shrivel up and die—not to mention the rest of his body. Wasn't hooking up supposed to be the best distraction from all the bullshit he was dealing with? But apparently, he couldn't even get that.

After a few minutes of fruitless messaging, he tossed the phone aside. Fine, then. If he couldn't find anybody, he'd just have to go for a run instead. At least that way he'd burn off a little of this nervous energy.

Out in the street, he set off on his usual route. He was still human for now, but as soon as he reached the park limits he'd shift. It was better to run like that. Human thoughts seemed to trouble you less. Technically, it wasn't exactly legal. Some humans were still threatened by seeing shifters in their wolf forms, and the park was supposed to be for everybody's use. In reality, however, it was a rule that was rarely enforced, especially after dark when all the humans stayed home, and the park transformed from an enclosed bit of green in the center of a city to the closest thing to wilderness that any of them had.

He'd prefer to go out to the real wilderness more often, but... damn. Who had the money to pay for that kind of non-essential travel?

He could run with confidence despite the quiet in the streets. A smaller, less physically capable person might have felt frightened of the violence that could happen out here, but Jake didn't need to worry about any of that. In truth, that only made him more frustrated with the nightmares he suffered from. What kind of weak asshole was he? He wasn't afraid of violent criminals, but the bad dreams he had in his own bed had him shaking so hard that he needed to leave the apartment and go.

It didn't make any sense.

Rather than focus on all this, he tried to think of the positives as his feet—both real and synthetic—pounded the pavement, muscles melting into the motions of physical activity. That, at least, was a comfort; he understood physical strain. It was the mental bullshit that had him pinned to the wall. But in the interests of trying his best, where were those positives?

Well, number one, he was awake early enough to beat the crowds. That meant he'd be able to hand his resume in at a good number of places before the city got too populated to be comfortable. He had ten print copies left, not including the original he used to make those copies whenever he had the spare change to make them. If he found any more places to apply, he'd just have to resort to giving out the handwritten ones.

He paused for a moment to let a car pass by, jogging on the spot rather than standing completely still. His mind wasn't busy enough yet; he'd only tie himself into knots if he gave himself the opportunity.

Okay. Positive number two.

His mind went blank. The city's nighttime silence made a mockery of him, staring back at him with no inspiration whatsoever.

Fine, he thought, falling back onto the usual ones. I'm not homeless yet. I'm alive. I have a prosthetic that fits. I can afford to pay my cell phone this month.

Having only these very basic things to rely on somehow made him feel worse. There was never any progression from them; there was never anything new to add to the list. Besides, he couldn't help but acknowledge the shadowy future in which they would no longer be true.

Then what would he lean on in his difficult times?

He shook his head, trying to push the thoughts aside and count his steps instead. Two, four, six, eight...

By the time he had worked up a sweat, the light was beginning to blush out over the tops of the buildings, and he figured it was time to head back. He could take a shower and head right back out again. Maybe try Grindr again this evening. Anything to keep that momentum going.

God only knew what he'd do if he had to stop.

Chapter Two

Mikhail

"Hey—buddy, I'm sorry, but you have to stop. No time for coloring right now! We have to leave for school."

"Already?"

Mikhail Debrov didn't consider himself to be a soft or weak-willed man, but his resolve nearly crumbled every single time Alexei looked at him like that. The kid was an absolute treasure. He wasn't badly behaved in the least—but he was quite a soft-hearted child, and going off to school with the rough and tumble of the other kids wasn't always easy for him. Seeing every bit of that nervousness in his son's eyes melted all the stiff seriousness in Mikhail's heart.

Granted, he never really felt very stiff or serious around his son in the first place—but the point still stood. In any case, it felt like they never got enough time together any more.

"I'm sorry, Alex," he said, genuinely meaning it. He squeezed the boy's shoulder, lifting the same hand to comb quickly through his son's white-blond hair. An inheritance from Mikhail himself. "Yes, already. It's a breakfast club morning, I'm afraid. I've got to get into the station."

"Can't I go with you?"

He leaned down to kiss the boy's head. "If you could, I'd take you," he promised. "But unfortunately, no kiddos allowed. You'll be okay at school, though, right? You can take your book of fairy tales to read before class."

Alexei shook his head—a hard 'no'.

"No to the book?" Mikhail prodded. "Or no to the fairy tales?"

Alex chewed the inside of his lip, not quite meeting his dad's eyes. It didn't feel good to see him like that. Far from it. Mikhail was a cop; if nothing else, shouldn't he fill his son with a feeling of protection that lasted even when they weren't beside each other? If Lorelei was still here, she'd know what to do.

But Lorelei hadn't been here for nearly two years now. Frankly, she hadn't been fully emotionally present even before she died—and admittedly, when it came to their relationship, neither had Mikhail.

Thinking of her was complicated. Unpleasant. He pushed away from her, abandoning the attempt to discern what she would do, and tried to make his own guesses instead.

"Is it the kids there?"

Alex paused, then nodded.

"They make fun of fairy tales?" Mikhail asked, adjusting his uniform in the mirror. If he had the time, all his attention would be on Alex; it wasn't without guilt that he had to divide it up between his son and getting ready for work. "Like their dad doesn't read to them at night, too."

"They say they don't," said Alexei, uncertain. Whether he was uncertain of their claim or his father's wasn't clear. "I don't want to read it there."

"Well, that's okay, bud," Mikhail assured him. "Don't ever do something you don't want to do on my account. I just thought you would want to read them; that's all."

He could sense sadness in the silence, and wished again that they had more time to explore this. As the only breadwinner in the family and with nobody around to help care for Alex, Mikhail simply didn't have any other option but to work long hours and try to balance everything as best he could. It wasn't the best-case scenario. It was the only scenario right now, at least until he could find a new partner.

If he ever did. If that was even an acceptable, moral thing to do.

"I do want to read them," Alex insisted, tugging on his dad's jacket. Mikhail looked down into his eyes, sensing the internal struggle that his young son was finding it hard to communicate. Of course he couldn't communicate it; he was so young. How were the kids in his class already so cruel to one another?

"I understand," Mikhail assured him. "You can keep them safe here at home, can't you? And then nobody can tell you anything about it."

Alex nodded, holding his dad's jacket in one hand. Mikhail made no move to extricate him, simply offering his hand once he was ready to leave and leading Alex out to the car.

"We'll read them together tonight," he suggested. "You can help me do the voices, can't you? You know all the words by now."

It wasn't much of a compliment in the grand scheme of things, but Alex seemed pleased enough by it—by being asked to help his dad with anything at all. He beamed up in Mikhail's direction, and it suddenly struck the cop that no matter how difficult his life was, every second of it was worth it for the moments that Alex found a reason to smile.

That, at least, he knew Lorelei would have approved of.

Of course, Lorelei was out of the picture now. What she did and did not approve of didn't really count, even if he felt guilt for thinking that. It was Alexei that mattered—even on the question of finding a new partner, too. Surely he would have some thoughts and feelings about the idea of sharing his dad with somebody else, even if Mikhail took great pains to ensure he was still taking great care of his baby? Even if this new woman was really nice?

There was little point in thinking about it now. After all, he was no closer to finding a new wife than he was to being the King of Spain, and these thoughts were only distracting him from this little slice of time he had with Alex this morning.

"You didn't tell me what went on at school yesterday, you know," he prompted, starting the engine. "What are you learning about right now?"

"History," said Alex, pronouncing the word as though it were a niche specialism. "And... Mrs. Winter wants us to talk about wolves in society."

Mikhail hummed quietly, not wishing to express his reservations in front of Alex. Their species was still downtrodden in society, and he knew that Alex's classmates certainly wouldn't treat him more kindly if they found out that he, too, was a wolf. Unless they already knew, somehow. "Yeah? Are you excited?"

"I want to know it all," said Alex. It sounded like he had reservations too. "Are they gonna make me tell?"

Well, there was that question answered. "Absolutely not," said Mikhail. "That's your secret, and you can keep it as long as you want." At least, they shouldn't. He was legally required to inform the school and Alex's teacher that they were dealing with a shifter, but equally, they were required not to disclose that information to the other students. For all Mikhail and Alex knew, the entire class was comprised of wolf cubs. Maybe it was better to think about it like that. If Alex was ever discovered, the alternative was... unpleasant.

All the same, he could imagine how his son felt. Mikhail had never been a wallflower in school; he had been eagerly involved with the rough and tumble of yard time, and never had any difficulty fitting in. Once he became a parent, though, he learned to read the concern and caution in Alexei's face; he absorbed it by osmosis, and began to know what it felt like to be excluded too.

"You're going to be fine, kid," he said into the silence. "It'll be cool to learn about people like us."

Alex nodded, but didn't answer.

In truth, Mikhail knew the day would soon come when his son expressed that he'd prefer to be normal. Other shifter parents had warned him that it would happen, and he was beginning to see it now. The sad part was that it wasn't crazy. It would be much easier to be a human instead of a shifter. Prejudice was rife in today's society, and holding that secret could be very damaging. Mikhail was lucky to have been hired as part of the police force's diversity program, and never had to hide himself from his employer.

There was every chance Alex wouldn't be so lucky when he grew up.

He leaned over to kiss his son's head as they pulled up outside the school. Someday soon, Alex would grow out of wanting affection from his dad; he'd pull away and wrinkle up his nose, telling Mikhail that he 'wasn't a baby'.

Thankfully, that day was not today. Alex's arms wrapped around his neck just like they did every day, squeezing him in a hug before quickly retreating. "Thanks, Dad."

"You take care of yourself today and behave for Mrs. Willis, okay? I'll see you tonight."

He watched Alex's progress across the road and into the school building. Knowing the rowdy crowd of kids that awaited him there, he wished that he could follow—but he didn't have time, and having his dad follow him into school probably wouldn't make things any better for Alex in the long run anyway. Watching from a distance was just part of the pain of being a parent.

Granted, most parents would be there to pick their kids up after school, but... that just wasn't an option for Alex and Mikhail. Not right now.

Mikhail only allowed himself a couple of seconds to feel bad about it before pulling away to head to work. This wasn't the time to get sad. After all, didn't he have a city to protect?

Chapter Three

Jake

"Alright," he heard himself say, for the thousandth time. "No problem. Thanks for your time."

Jake turned on his heel and headed out of the store before he had to look at the proprietor's accusatory face any longer. It was infuriating to hear his own polite tone of voice over and over again, making the same conciliatory 'thank yous', knowing that the second he left the store he'd be the topic of conversation between his point of contact and the rest of the staff.

Did that shifter really think we were going to hire them?

Or: I think that's the sketchiest job applicant we've ever had at the desk.

It was exhausting, and demoralizing, and it wasn't even lunchtime yet. Not that Jake had much to eat, but... the clock on the Warner building would chime out at midday just the same, and it didn't feel good to know that he'd made absolutely no progress all morning.

Unfortunately, it also wasn't a surprise. He was about as obvious a shifter as it was possible to be, with the tell-tale old scars of teenage fights across the bridge of his nose, and the single gold ring in his right earlobe. Every day he wrestled with taking that thing out for job-hunting, but what good would it do him to get a job with a prejudiced employer? Removing the traditional mark of an omega might conceal his identity in the short-term, but as soon as his colleagues or his boss found out the truth, he'd be back out on his ass and back at square one.

Might as well weed out the bigots before they could weed him out. If he got a job, he wanted it to be with somebody who knew exactly who he was. That way, they could never hold it against him.

He allowed himself a short break after this specific inquiry. The store manager he spoke to had been especially suspicious of him, and he could feel her eyes on him as he left—as though he'd spitefully shoplift something as revenge for being turned down on the way out of the place. He shook his head, taking a seat down at a public bench and massaging with strong hands at the connection between his leg and the prosthetic. It was sore to walk around this much, especially after a run this morning. Nothing he'd complain about aloud, but... damn, he felt like he was screwing his body up for no reason.

Not for the first time, his mind drifted to the big question. What was he going to do if this effort just... never paid off?

There were advocate groups and charities which helped shifters get work, but they weren't really a viable option for Jake. It had taken a long time—and a lot of foolish wounded pride—for him to approach the first one, only for them to wrinkle their noses at his history.

Sure, he knew it was harder to place someone with a criminal record, but wasn't increased juvenile criminality a shifters' rights issue too? All those bored kids traversing the streets with little to do except scrap with one another—with nothing but a bad reputation to live up to. Anyway, he was blatantly reformed now. By the military, no less.

Couldn't someone give him a second chance?

He saw a cop heading his way out of the corner of his eye. That kind of observation was a relic of his life as a criminal; he couldn't help noticing the police now, even when he was doing absolutely nothing wrong. He supposed it had to do with being a shifter, too. Sometimes he could be stopped and asked questions simply by virtue of his species. People were afraid of him, and sometimes cops were no exception.

Perhaps that was why he wasn't surprised when the cop continued in his direction, apparently heading right for him instead of walking past. If he was approached, it wouldn't be the first time or the last.

At least he didn't have anything on him, today. At least there was nothing he could reasonably be taken in for.

He looked up to meet the officer's eyes, cutting in before he could speak. "Can I help you, officer?" His tone was polite but confident—the air of a man who didn't mind being approached, but was altogether too used to the system that had you do so.

"It'd be helpful if we could talk, yes," said the officer. Well... that wasn't a bad start. Sometimes cops were offended when they could see they didn't intimidate you, as though your refusal to be afraid of them was some kind of insubordination in and of itself. This one didn't have that air about him. Besides, he was pretty nice to look at. He filled out the uniform nicely, with muscles that suggested he spent more time in the gym than the doughnut shop, and his white-blond hair was a severe contrast against the police navy.

Jake shifted aside, lifting his folder away from the bench so that there was space for the guy to sit down. "Be my guest."

"I'll stand, sir, if that's alright," said the cop. Of course. Wouldn't want to put yourself into a vulnerable position next to a dangerous shifter with a bunch of resumes in a manila wallet, would he? "I just need to ask you a few questions about this morning."

"Uh huh."

"We've had reports come in that you've been moving from store to store, one at a time down this street and... I believe also on 28th street. Is that correct?"

"That's correct, sir, yes."

The cop nodded, leaving a silent pause before realizing that Jake wasn't going to speak without being prompted. Jake had learned that particular lesson a long time ago. Offering information up without being asked for it could be perceived as guilt. He'd even seen a cop make that argument in court. Absolute nonsense, but... hey, if it helped him stay on the right side of a jail cell, Jake would stick to it.

"Would you mind telling me what you were doing? The store owner I spoke with said that you seemed to be scoping the place out."

"I'm looking for a job."

The officer blinked down at him. "A job."

"Yes, sir," said Jake, lifting the manila folder up again and offering it over. The officer took it, opening the front cover and flicking through the layers of paper in there. "So I've been going round to make inquiries, see. They don't always put help wanted ads in the window, and... y'know. Don't ask, don't get."

"Right," said the officer. He closed the folder, but didn't hand it back yet. "Only none of the people we spoke to mentioned that."

Jake lifted his hands in a shrug. He didn't want this cop to see him sweat, but... shit. Those assholes couldn't even tell the truth to a cop about what he was in for? Did he look that suspicious? "I don't know what to tell you, sir. That's what I've been doing."

"Did you hand any resumes out?"

"This morning? No. Nobody wanted to take one."

"Pity," said the cop. "Would've corroborated your story."

His tone of voice was strange. Jake couldn't tell whether the cop was being sarcastic, or whether he was genuinely on Jake's side, or whether he was advising him to ensure he left copies behind in the future, or... what. He furrowed his brow slightly, trying to read the face of this handsome cop standing before him.

"Guess so, but... that's life. I asked at every desk. Maybe you could... I don't know. Check CCTV, or something? Maybe somebody has audio."

I shouldn't be doing your job for you. He leaned back into the bench, already tired of this conversation. He wished he'd never stopped to take a break. If he had gone straight on to the next store, then the cop might have heard him ask for work out loud, and then none of this would be an issue. Instead, here they were.

"Okay," said the cop, after a pause. "Let me call in at some of these stores and talk to the people there, see what they have to say. Are you going to stick around here, or do I need a colleague to come and sit with you?"

Jake looked away, shoving his hands into his pockets. Fucking cops. Any approval he might have felt for this one was fast fading. Why did they have to treat him like a criminal, even now? No wonder he'd gone so haywire as a kid if they were going to act the same however he behaved. "I'm not going to make a run for it, officer. I haven't done anything wrong."

Besides, you've got my resumes.

"Alright. Five minutes."

True to his word, the cop was back before long. Jake didn't look up at his face—just kept track of him out of the corner of his eye. He didn't want to see the surprise on the guy's face to find Jake still sitting there. It'd only irritate him.

"Okay, sir," he said, reaching the bench. "Seems they just neglected to mention to us what you said when you approached them."

"Uh-huh."

"I'm sure this is frustrating for you, but it's important that we protect the community by following up reports of suspicious activity around the area."

"I don't think I was being suspicious," said Jake, thin on patience. "I walked right up to the desk, asked a polite professional question, and then walked out again."

"I'm only following up reports, sir."

"Well, how do you suggest I act?" said Jake, finally turning to meet the cop's eyes. He saw a steady gaze looking back at him—strong and non-violent, but very hard to read. There certainly wasn't any sympathy in there. Jake couldn't help but feel frustrated. "Should I ask them not to call the cops on me as I'm leaving? Because in my mind that would be suspicious."

"I'm not accusing you of anything, sir."

"Alright," Jake said with a faint laugh, shaking his head down at the bench. "Thanks for not accusing me."

The cop stayed silent. Jake could feel his blood boiling, and at the same time felt the cold prickle of his logical side needling at him. It was stupid to vent his frustration at this cop. It wouldn't make any difference, aside from maybe getting him noted down as a suspicious character. Then they really would keep stopping him.

Finally, after an age, the cop opened his folder of resumes again.

"I'll need to take one of these for my records."

Jeez. What a jobsworth. If this was really a non-incident, why did they need to back it up with any paperwork?

"Right," said Jake, rubbing at his leg and then standing from the bench at long last. "Well... make it a handwritten one, will you? I can't spare the print copies."

"I think a print one would-"

"Fine," Jake interrupted, holding up his hands and turning away. "Fine. Take a print one. Doesn't matter. Not like I'm swimming in offers anyway." Had he really spent money on photocopies of this damn resume only for one to end up in a shitty cop file? He hadn't done anything wrong.

He took the file as the cop offered it back. When he looked up to meet the guy's eyes with irritable defiance, he still only saw a cool, blank look there. He couldn't imagine wanting to stop innocent people like this for a living.

"This says you're a veteran," said the cop, folding the resume. "Is that correct?"

So now I'm guilty of stolen valor too? Is that it?

"That's correct," he said, thin-lipped.

The cop nodded, giving the paper one more look before placing it inside his notebook and closing it firmly. "Well, thank you for your service, and your time. Have a good day, sir."

"Yeah. Thanks," said Jake, unable to weed all the sarcasm out. He headed off down another street, tired of looking at this one for the day. He could finish hitting the rest of the stores here tomorrow. If he saw that cop once more, good for nothing except for looking at, Jake wasn't sure he'd ever sleep tonight from the frustration.

Not that he slept well to begin with.

Chapter Four

Mikhail

As a consummate professional, it was extremely rare for any police case to get under Mikhail's skin. After all, at 32, he had been in this job for a decade now. He had seen too much for anything to be shocking. Yet here he was unable to get that scruffy-looking shifter Jake Frost out of his head.

Things between them had started out fairly amicably. Jake was evidently quite used to being approached by cops, and as such wasn't intimidated by it. Only when Mikhail pressed the issue and made all of the appropriate checks did he begin to get frustrated—and in truth, Mikhail could kind of understand that. If the guy had really only been looking for a job, which it seemed like he had been, then of course it would be frustrating to have a cop interfere with your business. To have twitchy human store-owners call the cops on you, and neglect to mention the innocuous nature of your visit as they made that report.

It probably didn't help that Mikhail didn't look like a shifter. Where Jake wore his omega's earring with pride, and had those dignified shifter scratches across his nose, Mikhail could easily pass for human. Until he got into heat and the natural identifying hormones kicked in, neither humans nor shifters could detect his species. That made for overhearing some interesting conversations between bigoted humans—but it also meant he could understand why humans were afraid of shifters. He saw the malice in some shifters' face as he approached them.

Humans treated shifters very badly, but frightened animals are always the most dangerous. Humans were no exception to that rule.

With Jake likely making the assumption that Mikhail was a human, and just perpetuating the harassment, it was no wonder he got annoyed. Still, Mikhail wished that he hadn't. Humans only got more nervous when they saw you react that way, not less nervous—and the more nervous they were around you, the worse things got. Besides, surely he had to know that the police had procedures to follow? That Mikhail wouldn't be doing his job correctly if he didn't follow up those complaints, regardless of how he personally felt about them?

No matter how many different calls he attended and how many people he helped, he still found his mind returning to those dark, smoky eyes and tousled brown hair—the tired and turbulent look on Jake's face. Something was still scratching at Mikhail, and he didn't know what it was.

Only when he reached the station to complete some paperwork did he make the connection.

He had to walk by the 'problem cases' board in the community office for the memory to click. Though it was long-gone now, he suddenly recalled seeing Jake's face staring out at him from that same wall. A gaunt and unflattering shot taken from grainy CCTV after he had been involved with a car theft.

Mikhail's jaw clenched, and his fist tightened around his notebook—and therefore around the resume folded up inside it.

That was why he hadn't been able to get Jake out of his head all day. Some part of him knew that Jake wasn't being straight-up with him. That Jake was, on some level, a criminal. He probably wasn't really a veteran, either.

"Hey," came a voice from behind him, followed by a soft hand on his shoulder. His colleague Jennifer—and exactly the kind of calming influence he needed right now. "You just walked straight past me with a face like thunder. I believe that makes it my responsibility to ask you what's wrong."

"Do I have the responsibility to answer?"

"Technically, no, but... it'll be better for you if you do."

She grinned, and though no part of Mikhail felt like smiling right now, he found himself mirroring her expression. Jennifer was a fairly new officer, and technically his junior—but her confidence and capability had fast transformed her into a colleague who Mikhail could really count on, and who he considered a real friend. Ordinarily, he would've been happy to trust her with his troubles.

Today, though? This felt like a strangely in-house issue for shifters only. As far as he knew, Jennifer was human—and the fact that they hadn't even had this conversation yet was a reason to sidestep the whole issue altogether.

"I'm just... my typically grouchy self," Mikhail said, brain hunting back for some evidence to hand over. It didn't take long to find some. "I think my son might be having a hard time with some of the kids at school, and I'd like to be there to pick him up from school, but..."

She winced, sympathetic. As far as Mikhail knew, Jennifer had no children, but maybe the sensation of wanting to protect somebody you loved was universal enough to cover the gap between a parent and not-a-parent. "I'm sorry. Poor Alex." Her attention to detail was in her favor, and won major points; people didn't usually remember his son's name. The fact that she was invested enough to do so was pleasant. "He's such a sweet little kid. School's so tough."

"It is," Mikhail agreed. "That's the hard part, I guess. He's just not cut out for the kind of roughhousing the other kids his age like, and... what am I supposed to do? Suggest he change everything about himself to have an easier time? I don't know..."

Maybe this issue had been coloring his mood all day without him realizing it. As he began to speak about it now, so much was pouring out that he didn't even have to think about. The fact that any of his time had been devoted to Jake Frost at all kind of irritated him, with this putting it all into perspective.

"I'm sure his teachers are looking out for him," Jennifer pointed out. "Alex is adorable, and they know the warning signs. Maybe you could arrange to call them during the day or something? They might even be available right now. You could just... talk to them. Get them to keep a close eye."

"Yeah," he agreed, scrubbing a hand over his jaw thoughtfully. "Yeah, I think I'll have to do that. Thanks."

"You're welcome," she said, folding her arms. "And here I was, about to tell you off for looking mad. I'm gonna have to scrap that idea; I think I'd look just as mad if I was worried about something like that."

"Well, I'm glad I have your approval."

She smiled as she headed away to continue about her day. Not for the first time, Mikhail wondered whether she might not be a good partner. It didn't take long for him to realize that she was too young, and likely not a shifter. Besides, he'd never really felt that way about her, and he was pretty sure she didn't feel that way either. It was just the loneliness striking out and trying to examine every option, holding up every woman in his life to see if she might fill the gap that Lorelei left. The gap that Lorelei had left even when she was still alive.

Mikhail continued on to his office, his mind slowly drifting back to the Jake Frost problem now that he and Jennifer had talked the bullying one over. It was still irritating that this should be an issue in the first place, but... it wasn't like he could drive over to the elementary school and protect his son. Maybe Alex didn't need that anyway. It was just as Jennifer said—the teachers had been doing this long enough to know what it looked like when kids were being shitty to each other. He should just trust them to do their jobs, and be ready to help if things didn't resolve themselves.

It wasn't as though he had time to be more proactive about it.

Slipping into his desk chair with a frown on his face, Mikhail slipped the resume Jake had given him out of the notebook and read over it again. There it was—the claim that he was a veteran. Would the armed forces even accept a recruit with a criminal record like Jake's? Mikhail couldn't remember the details of what Jake had done, exactly, but for him to appear on that wall of troublemakers, he must have been fairly prolific as a petty criminal.

He drummed his fingers against the desk, and only took a few seconds to make a decision. He was going to need to look up Jake's file.

It was easy enough to search the database—and sure enough, there was Jake's extremely spotty record. Petty thefts. Fighting in the street. Possession of illegal substances. Everything you'd expect to see from the kind of asshole shifter stereotype that showed up on human soap operas to screw innocent women and cause a load of trouble.

The kind of stereotype that made life difficult for good shifters. The kind that made kids like Alex afraid to be outed at school.

Mikhail gritted his teeth, stood up from his desk, and made the immediate decision to head back out onto the street.

This was perhaps not the most professional course of action. There was, of course, a chance that Jake was out committing crimes now, and that returning to apprehend him would prevent those crimes. On that level, it was acceptable—but in truth, this wasn't about that. This was about the personal affront that Mikhail felt. About the lies. About the mixed feelings of guilt and fixation that he had felt, and that Jake had inspired.

It took a while for Mikhail to reach the street where he'd first found Jake. Of course, it had been several hours, and the omega was unlikely to be there anymore, but perhaps he'd still be in the same area. If he was committing crimes, he probably stuck to the same hunting ground that he was already familiar with. If that was the case, then Mikhail ought to find him quite quickly.

Unfortunately, if he was still sticking to the job-seeking story, then he might be casing out stores several blocks away by now—in any direction.

Frustrated, Mikhail headed down streets at random to patrol for answers. It seemed like overkill to head into businesses and ask for sighting confirmations. He didn't have a photograph to show them in any case, so it would all be guesswork and assumptions and...

He frowned, ears catching the conversation of two passersby on instinct.

"...don't know; a car backed up halfway down the street and he completely lost it."

"He was such a big guy, too. Looked like a shifter."

"I'll say..."

"Excuse me, ma'am," said Mikhail, cutting in. What did they mean, he 'lost it'? "Did something happen?"

"Oh!" The woman patted her chest with her hand. "You scared me, young man. Nothing happened, really—just a guy down there started freaking out a short while ago."

"Freaking out...?"

"A car backed up," said her friend. "A loud bang, you know? And he just went to pieces, like it was the scariest thing that ever happened to him."

Recognizing the description of a panic attack, perhaps related to PTSD, Mikhail's focus immediately shifted. "Thank you," he said, already setting off with his finger pointed down the street. "This way?"

"That's right."

He took off at a half-sprint, mindful of the fact that this person must feel very alone right now—that they needed his help. Police-work wasn't all about preventing crime, after all. Sometimes you were just there for help and for guidance, and if that was what this maybe-shifter needed right now...

He saw a hunched-over form at the edge of the street, and made for it blindly. No doubt, the figure was tall. The women he'd passed weren't wrong. It was kind of strange to see a tall guy crouched over in fear in public like this. Not funny, though. Quite the opposite. It was so contrary to expectations that for a few seconds he didn't even notice that he recognized the figure. That it belonged to exactly the same person as he'd been looking for.

"Alright, Jake," he said, voice low and calming, and fighting off his surprise. He crouched down beside him. "A car backed up, that's all. You're okay. Alright? You're okay."

Chapter Five

Jake

He felt cold, even though the day was fairly temperate. It had been at least twenty minutes since it happened now, and it was worth repeating that he'd never been in any danger in the first place. It had just been a loud noise that set him off. A noise like an explosion right beside him. The kind he had lost his leg to.

It didn't feel good to react that strongly. It didn't feel good to be sitting down drinking coffee he couldn't afford beside this interfering cop.

Unfortunately, he figured that he didn't have a choice right now. He did need to calm down, and the warm coffee was helping. Besides, the cop did seem to be at least trying to be kind. He'd bought the coffee, after all. Maybe he wasn't all bad. Just a jobsworth who didn't mind legitimizing and enforcing anti-shifter bigotry.

Okay, that wasn't such a small thing.

"You starting to feel a little better?" the officer asked.

"Sure."

It'd be rude to say 'no', wouldn't it? In any case, there wasn't really anything else that the officer could do to help. This wasn't an issue of logic, and the fear couldn't be explained away. It had to leave his body of its own accord over time, as all his individual systems learned one by one that he wasn't about to die. That nobody around him was about to die.

The war may have taken his leg, but this was worse by far. Worse even than the nightmare which stemmed from the same paranoia and fear. At least he had nightmares in private. Out here, he could feel a thousand different eyes staring at him. He didn't feel dignified, let alone safe.

"I had a friend come back just the same," the officer said into the silence. "I don't know what it's like. I can't imagine. But... I do understand."

Jake held his tongue, still wary of this authority figure who had only shown his morality in the face of absolute necessity. He was handsome, but that only meant that Jake had to be more guarded against him. Had to deliberately set his thinking in the opposite direction. Had to practically hate him.

He was probably straight anyway.

"Are you seeing anybody about this?" the officer ventured. "Are you... on any medication, or...?"

"I don't think you're allowed to ask me that."

The officer nodded slowly, holding up his hands. "No. You're right. I'm sorry. I'm just... concerned."

Jake looked him in the eyes for a few moments, trying to work him out. Was he really concerned? If so, what stopped him from being concerned about prejudice earlier today? What made him start caring now?

"I'm a big boy," Jake said eventually, picking his coffee up again. "I can take care of myself more often 'n not."

"I believe it, but we all need help sometimes."

The silence grew again, awkward and uncomfortable. After a long few beats, the officer gave in, apparently not quite as gifted as Jake was at dealing with the quiet. "Well—look. Maybe I should introduce myself. I'm Mikhail Debrov. This is my assigned area, so I patrol here quite often; if you do pick up work around here, I'll probably see you around a fair bit."

Jake snorted. "You think I'm likely to get a job here?"

"Why not?"

"You know why not."

Officer Debrov shook his head. "Earlier today? That was a fluke. I mean... anti-shifter sentiment isn't that bad here."

"Are you serious?" Jake knew his tone of voice was rude, but he couldn't help feeling incredulous. Not that bad? They called the cops on him for... well. Existing, he guessed. "Half the people I spoke to yesterday were afraid of me. The other half were passive-aggressive. If I was smaller or skinnier I don't know how they'd have treated me."

"I think if you were smaller or skinnier they might not have been intimidated," the officer pointed out. "I'm not saying they're right, but... people have ideas about shifters and how dangerous they are. If they don't think they're in any physical danger..."

"Then they probably won't be nervous about telling somebody innocent to go fuck themselves."

There was one thing Jake had to hand to Officer Debrov. He didn't flinch at the way Jake spoke to him. He didn't seem like the type to make an arrest because Jake was being a little abrupt with him. That wasn't always something you could take for granted, especially as a shifter. Another guy might have hauled him into a cell for just for swearing.

"I know where you're coming from," said Debrov. "Trust me. And I know getting hired is hard to begin with but... somebody round here is going to take you on sometime. Whether they recognize your value right away or whether they have to feel like they're taking a chance on you, I don't know, but... it'll happen."

Jake wrinkled his nose, looking away. "You might not think that way if you'd been looking as long as I have."

"Well, I'm sorry to hear that."

The following silence wasn't as bad as the others. There was at least a small kernel of understanding growing between them, and it gave Jake the patience to sit beside him without resenting it. The space to acknowledge that it was really kind of Officer Debrov to buy him this coffee. It went way beyond the scope of his official responsibilities and ventured into pure mortal kindness.

"I've got to admit," said the officer, into the silence. "I was actually out here looking for you when I ran into you. I realized that I recognized you, from... uh. A couple of years back. From the station wall..."

He trailed off, but he didn't need to finish the sentence. Jake already knew exactly what he meant. The part of him that had begun to feel a little warmer towards the officer felt a little threatened by it and bristled. What was the officer's point here?

"A record like yours, I was... kind of dubious about your claim to being a veteran."

The blond spoke like this was a confession of a mild mistake, but it struck Jake like a slap in the face. This was all even worse than he thought. He was right; the officer had been accusing him of stolen valor when he remarked on the references to being a veteran in his resume. What right did this asshole have to question the veracity of his service?

"I know; I know," said Debrov, holding up a hand to try and placate the angry look on Jake's face. It didn't work. "I shouldn't have made that assumption. I guess I just... didn't understand how a criminal record like that could lead to the army. Maybe that response is why employers are having a hard time picturing you in their businesses."

"That's a crock of shit."

He knew he was risking a lot speaking to an officer of the law like this, but he couldn't contain his frustration.

"Jake-"

"It's Mr. Frost," said Jake, cutting in. "A judge ordered me to join the army to straighten me out. It worked. No matter what happened, there's nothing in my life I'm more grateful for than the opportunity to serve. And you thought I lied about it to try and get a job stacking shelves in some third-rate store?"

"I did acknowledge that it was a mistake."

"But you were going to interrogate me about it," Jake continued. "If you hadn't seen me like you did, you would have forced me to prove it."

"Surely you can understand why it would be an issue for people to be parading around claiming military history they didn't have, and-"

"And I'm sure it is an issue," said Jake, hotly. "Except I'm not a liar."

He reached down to lift his trouser leg, exposing a thin metal strip of the prosthetic beneath—the most expensive thing he owned, and the item that had taken most sacrifice to acquire it. He felt no shame showing it to the officer, or to anybody. Even when he saw the hint of pity in Officer Debrov's face, he kept his white-hot resolve.

"I know you're not a liar," the cop insisted, voice calm and soft. Frustratingly so, compared to the strength of feeling that Jake was experiencing—but of course none of this mattered to him. He'd go back to his shift and be paid for it; he'd leave to a home he owned pretty securely at night, and curl up next to his wife, and... Jake grimaced, looking away. The bastard didn't know how lucky he was, and still he was talking as though he had something to offer Jake. "All I mean to say is that... you've obviously come a long way, Mr. Frost, but you don't help yourself."

"Excuse me?"

"Shifter prejudice is a real thing," Officer Debrov continued. "You've seen it. I've seen it. It's real. It's disgusting, but we all have to live with it. Sometimes the best thing you can do for yourself is to work hard to defy all the stereotypes. With respect, sir, you do look like you might intimidate a bigoted human. They don't understand how wrong that is, but they're going to feel it anyway. Can't you try to appease them, even just for your own sake if not theirs?"

Jake couldn't believe his ears, or his eyes. He shook his head, a smile on his face that had nothing to do with happiness or amusement. No positive emotion whatsoever.

"Y'know what?" he said, standing from his seat. "Thanks for the coffee. Officer. The bullshit advice, I could do without."

"I wasn't trying to offend you..."

But Jake had no time for any of this. Not any longer. He didn't turn back as he left the coffee store, ignoring the looks from the staff. They'd never have let him inside this place if he hadn't been with the officer—so doubtless, he'd never be able to return again. Whatever. The last thing he needed was this kind of society. The kind that expected him to look human or starve.

Fuck. He'd rather starve, if that was the standard. He'd rather shift and run wild, abandoning the human world entirely.

His animal instinct was raging. In fact, the thought of shifting had him in a frenzy. Grindr may be a wash, but maybe running in the fields would be a decent alternative tonight. Maybe there was somebody else frantic and frustrated just like him. Even if there wasn't, he could do with the rush of adrenaline to keep him alive.

God only knew there was very little else going for him today.

Chapter Six

Mikhail

The conversation had clearly not gone well.

Driving home from work, a few hours had already passed since Jake walked away from him, and Mikhail still felt bad about it. No matter what Jake may have assumed about Mikhail and his intentions, he only wanted the best for the younger shifter—and for society in general. The police were undoubtedly an imperfect institution, but Mikhail had stepped into policing to try and diversify it. To uphold the voices of shifters and to combat the kind of prejudice and bigotry that Jake had experienced today.

Surely that didn't mean that it was wrong to try and game the system? Sure, it sucked that you had to act like a human to get gainful employment, but... if that was what it took, then there was no shame in doing so. No shame in taking that earring out.

It made logical sense. So why was he clenching the steering wheel so tightly, with ripples of guilt loosening and tightening his fingers in waves?

None of it mattered any longer, anyway. He was heading home to Alexei. Unfortunately, it probably wouldn't count for much, as the kid was probably already asleep—or at least he would soon be getting there. This had been a long shift today. At least they'd managed to have a little conversation this morning before school, but it didn't make Mikhail feel any less guilty about being absent from his son's childhood.

What kind of sense did it make that he'd wasted time today having Jake bristle at him when he could've been reading with Alex? Of course, everybody needed money to live off of, and single-parent families more so than any other, but... as he headed through the door now, it didn't feel right.

"Hey—sorry, I'm..."

He silenced himself as he stepped into the sitting room, seeing that Mrs. Willis had already fallen asleep on the couch. It wasn't that late, but... well. She was an older lady, after all. Mrs. Willis was kind of like an aunt to both Mikhail and to Alex, and he wasn't sure how they'd get by without her. It wouldn't be the first time she had slept in their place instead of her own home a few doors down. Still, he hoped that she was comfortable, and carefully pulled a blanket up over her.

Frustration was still heavy in him. Even once he'd stuck his head inside Alexei's bedroom door, seeing his favorite person fast asleep, he only felt a little better. Thankfully, Mikhail knew what this kind of restlessness meant.

He needed to shift, and to run—and it wasn't too late for it, either.

It didn't take him long to reach the running grounds. Like many shifters, Mikhail had deliberately chosen a home within walking distance of them, knowing how terrible the desperation to shift could feel—knowing that the penalties for shifting among humans could be terrible, both officially and unofficially. In fact, living within a short distance of the city's running grounds was one of the key ways to work out who was a shifter and who wasn't. Only the fact that housing was cheaper around the grounds prevented you from knowing entirely; some humans were forced to live here for financial reasons alone.

It didn't take a bitter soul like Jake to see how unkindly those humans regarded shifters. Prejudice wasn't entirely in his head.

Mikhail shook his own head as he reached the entrance of the grounds, shaking out his limbs too to try and stave off the adrenaline. He didn't want to think of today at all when he did this. He wanted to be as free mentally as he was physically.

Only once he had his mind clear and his body pulsing with need did he finally let his form go—and shift.

His paws hit the ground with force, falling straight into a sprint across the rolling grass. He should probably have waited for his fur to fully grow in and for his senses to settle first, but he didn't have the patience right now. He needed the wind coursing against him, and the dense woodland where most of his fellow wolves spent the night. Being alone was calming in this form too, but there was something healing about being around other wolves, unaware of who they were in their human form—somehow both familial and anonymous.

You could feel these roles instinctively. Mikhail knew one as soon as he came into contact with his first wolf. This was brother, or as close to it as he could come; he charged into the strange wolf with playful force, and for a few minutes enjoyed the non-malicious tussle of a play-fight, as wild and unworried as if he were a cub. Neither wolf lost, and neither wolf won; when they parted, breath heaving and scattering off in opposite directions, there was a mutual feeling of satisfaction it would be impossible to get as a human.

Things were just different in this form. Less angry—less constrained. More real.

He passed another few wolves out in the woods. He recognized none of them; after all, there were enough wolves in this city to fill a thousand packs. Thankfully, he didn't need to recognize them in order to feel comforted by their presence.

Before long, however, he became aware of a much different presence in his general area. He paused in his run, paws padding to a halt on the cool patchy grass, and peered sideways into the trees. Many meters away, he could see the glint of another wolf's eyes. An omega. He could sense it as easily as he could sense the species, and his own attraction to this wolf. What surprised him, a heartbeat later, was that it was a male.

That had never happened before.

He took a few hesitant steps in the omega wolf's direction, feeling the shuddering desire grow in him from the base of his spine all the way through to his sexual center. The omega didn't move or break his eye contact, staring him down as if daring him to come closer. Challenging him to come closer. It was a challenge Mikhail couldn't resist. Only today, he'd been thinking about how lonely he was, and here was the first kindred spirit to stir him in a very long time.

Male or female, he couldn't ignore that pull. He was much too desperate.

Besides—what did it really matter, anyway?

Certain of what he wanted now, he took a few more deliberate steps in the omega's direction. All of a sudden, the strange omega took off—and Mikhail followed by instinct, paws thundering against the ground with no desire to slow or give up the chase. He could practically feel the other wolf's laughter, beckoning him from way ahead. Then, from closer. In fact, Mikhail felt himself closing the gap faster than he expected to. Only as he rounded on the omega did he notice that one of his back legs was missing.

That didn't make any difference, either.

He snapped playfully at the omega, catching and tumbling him over into the undergrowth nearby. They weren't the only ones in the forest, but it felt like they were; as they play-fought, intentions far lustier than they had been with the brother-wolf, everything else in the city vanished. No prejudice—no police-work keeping him away from his son.

He nosed down at the omega's belly, as confident in the omega's attraction to him as he was confident of his own desire. It was just blatantly mutual, even with the omega's feistiness and dark, daring eyes.

He let the omega up, faces pressing together in a silent communication of what would soon follow. Sure enough, when the omega took off again, it was not at full speed—they were searching for a place together, no longer requiring the pretense of chasing and catching. The deal was done.

In the dark, there was no need for romance or conversation. The omega shifted to human form and out of his clothes, already on his knees; Mikhail moved in place behind him, hand stroking over the small of his strange omega's broad, muscular back. It felt surprisingly normal to be preparing to fuck a man, for saying Mikhail had never experienced this type of attraction before.

He presumed the stranger's familiar scent was recognizable largely because of its masculinity—similar to his own scent in a way that a woman's never could be.

They had never met before. Right?

Mikhail spat into his hand and slid his hand down the stranger's ass, fingers feeling for the tight, hot opening that he knew he'd find there. This would be rough, but that was the kind of sex shifters came here for. If they were seeking romantic kisses and satin-slick luxury, they'd be looking for a date. Running was about spontaneity and dirt and rawness; none of that changed when running together turned into sex.

A little pain could go hand in hand with pleasure.

He could hear the omega grunting underneath him, face turned down against the grass and ass pushed up, back arched and eager for what Mikhail had to give him. He dutifully added a second finger, carefully bent and slowly working in and out to open the stranger up. Only when he couldn't take it anymore did he shuffle forward, cock already hard and seeping wet at the head.

With a grunt, he pushed hard inside the stranger, delighting in the satisfied groan it elicited. It made him feel big—made him feel good and in control, as any alpha should. He rocked his hips forward, giving the omega only a second or so to adjust before fucking into him in earnest, hissing and moaning at the tight heat he found there.

The forest around them was quiet, offering only a background of whispering leaves and distant howls as a backdrop to their incoherent groaning. Mikhail felt no desire to speak except to swear, his tone quiet and coarse as he came close to finishing. Even then, as he peaked and came inside the strange omega, he didn't announce it—just gripped the man's hips tight, nails digging into the soft skin of his body, and rode out the wave of pleasure. Felt the rhythmic clenching of the stranger's ass as he came too.

He pulled out silently, slipping to the ground beside the omega and brushing off his knees. With his human eyes adjusting slowly to the dark—well, it was hard for them to adjust while they were squeezed shut in pleasure—he could just about make out the mound of his clothes a meter away, barely able to structure the memory of taking them off.

"Rough day?" asked the stranger, his own voice rough too but laced with amusement. Clearly, this wasn't a criticism or a complaint. Far from it.

"You could say that," said Mikhail, finally looking sideways to take in the human appearance of the omega he'd fucked.

That was when the bottom just about fell out of his stomach.

"Wait..."

Jake Frost finally looked up at him, his dark eyes full of a new sensuality far different from the anger and frustration they had worn earlier today. For what it was worth, he did seem surprised—though he was holding onto himself much better than Mikhail had, with only a slow blink and a lazy smile to betray himself.

"Well, shit," he said eventually, running a hand through his hair and flopping down onto the grass. "I thought you were human—never mind like this..."

Mikhail pulled a knee up to his chest, head reeling and unsure where he stood now. He didn't know what to say. Having fucked Jake like this, wild and unconstrained, he felt he'd stumbled into something deeply intimate. He was unprepared for what that felt like, and the intensity of it.

After a few moments of silence, Jake sighed and reached over for his pants—not without difficulty. He seemed sore, and with a bashful flush, Mikhail realized exactly why.

"It's fine. Secret's safe with me," said Jake, his voice back to business now, and sitting up straight on the ground. There was a trace of the old irritation there. "I guess I learned my lesson, too. You're not as straight-laced as you look. Might want to be careful with that."

"I, uh..."

"It's fine," Jake repeated, holding up a hand as he slipped on his pants, and then pulled his shirt on over his head. Mikhail's eye caught on the empty pant leg where his missing leg would've been. How hadn't he realized when he saw the wolf was missing one? In any case, he turned back to Jake's face. "I'll still think of you as a professional jackass and I'll forget you ever fucked me. So you don't have to feel bad about doing the same."

"I mean, I..."

But Mikhail didn't get a chance to finish his sentence. With that, Jake shifted back to his wolf form, scampering away into the woods far more easily on three legs than he could have on one. Mikhail was left to frown into the darkness, his clothes around his feet, and wonder whether this was the outcome he wanted, or whether he would have preferred the messy, roguish omega to curl up and stay. The answer wasn't as clear as he once might have guessed.

Chapter Seven

Jake

He was sore all over his body. It was early afternoon already, and he didn't really feel much better than he had in the morning—but Jake wouldn't trade that just-fucked feeling for the world. Even if it had been a one-time encounter that he absolutely couldn't repeat, there was a sick kind of satisfaction in deriving his pleasure from someone like Mikhail.

The guy had seemed pretty screwed up when he realized who Jake was. Was he usually straight, Jake wondered? Or was he just scum in Mikhail's law-abiding eyes? Either way, he quite liked the idea of being a source of regret for the asshole.

That's what he told himself, anyway. The pinch of regret at the thought of never screwing like that again was easy enough to ignore. After all, he was still looking for a job; that took way more energy than daydreaming about muscular alphas fucking him into the ground in the running fields darkness.

It wasn't like he wanted or needed anybody, anyway.

Rubbing at the base of his back as though that would ease the pain, he took a deep breath and headed into the bakery that was next on his job-hunting list. It was a busy time; the elementary school a street or so away seemed to have just kicked out, and there were a whole bunch of parents and students milling about the place together. Ordinary job-hunters might think of this as a bad time to inquire, but Jake figured he couldn't have any worse luck than he already had. Besides, maybe seeing the place so packed out would remind the proprietor exactly how much they needed to hire a little more help.

That was the theory, anyway.

The moment he actually entered the little bakery, he felt the same air of suspicion he had experienced the other day. It wasn't anything in particular that made him feel that way. Nobody said anything rude to him—at least not yet. Nobody outright stared. He could just feel eyes on him, and tense body language on every side. As he approached the desk, he could see the manager there drawing herself up as if preparing for a fight.

He might as well just walk away right now, but his pride wouldn't allow it. Besides, he was here to ask for a job. Jake had no intention of letting them believe their assumptions about him had been right. If there was any chance of them feeling guilty once they realized he was totally innocuous and safe, then he wanted to take that chance.

"Hi there," he said, voice totally professional and polite. Irritated as he was that their shackles were already up, he didn't want to show it. "I was just wondering whether you're hiring at the moment."

The woman raised her eyebrows at him. "Really?"

"Sure," said Jake, fighting to keep his cool. Stay calm. There's no need to stoop to her level. "Sorry—did I miss a 'help wanted' card in the window...?"

"There's no card," she said, eyes still wide and unfriendly. "That isn't what I meant."

He didn't want to let her get away with it this easily. If she wanted to be a gross bigot, then she was going to have to speak her prejudice out loud—not just imply it and pretend to be a good person with alternative motives. His silence hung in the air as he waited for her to explain, hearing the bell of the door as it opened behind him.

"You know, there's an elementary school right down the street," said the manager, pretending to look at something on her desk. At least, Jake presumed that she was pretending; her eyes didn't move as they would if she was actually examining something. "I have to make sure that this is a school-friendly environment."

"I'm pretty good with kids," Jake said, content to play the role of an innocent man unaware of her bias. Go ahead and just say it. "And I feel my time in the army gave me a great sense of integrity that could really work for a school environment."

"I just don't think parents would really like it."

"A veteran?"

She tightened her lips, trying to think of another way to say it. As she glanced over his shoulder, however, he could see the relief in her eyes. "Oh—Officer Debrov. Good afternoon, sir."

Seriously?

Jake turned on his heel, giving Mikhail an incredulous smile. "If I didn't know better, I might think you were following me."

The alpha actually flushed, but managed a faint smile. Before Mikhail could answer, the owner of the bakery spoke again. "Has this man been causing trouble, officer?"

"What makes you ask?"

She glanced between them, as if surprised that Mikhail couldn't see what she was talking about. Clearly, she expected the police to be as anti-shifter as she was. She probably had experience with officers that were eager to back that belief up. "Well..."

"Just looking for a job," said Jake. His eyes returned to Mikhail's. See? I told you so. He felt more comfortable and defiant around the cop now that they'd slept together in the running fields. Jake felt he'd seen a side of Mikhail that even he hadn't known about until it happened. "I guess I'm not a suitable candidate."

"There's no opening anyway," the owner insisted, but Jake could see the understanding in Mikhail's eyes. For the first time, he felt lucky that they had met one another in the street. He felt that something good might come out of it, or that Mikhail might actually believe him. "I've already asked him to leave."

"You didn't," said Jake, non-combative but quite certain.

"I implied it."

"Mrs. Kelly," said Mikhail, keeping a steady tone. "I'm sure Jake is happy to leave if he's done anything to upset you. He's quite an upstanding guy."

"I'm sure," she said, half-scoffing.

"Excuse me?"

Jake blinked, surprised to hear Mikhail reply to her that way. So far, he'd kept his cool, and he seemed to want to believe that nobody was bigoted unless they outright said 'I hate shifters'. What was making him so proactive about challenging this lady now?

"Well... officer, you know how it is."

"You'll have to tell me."

She glanced between Jake and Mikhail, suspicious now. "You know. His... kind."

For the first time, Jake noticed the tiny blond boy holding Mikhail's hand—and only now because he flinched as Mrs. Kelly spoke. Jake knew that feeling. The sensation of hearing somebody who you once liked say something so disgusting about you and your species. The poor kid.

"I'm sorry, Mrs. Kelly, but I hope you're not referring to his species."

She wrinkled her nose. "They're dangerous. Everyone knows that—you too, even if you have to act politically correct. Would you really want one around Alex?"

Jake turned back to the boy. His big, blue eyes were as wide as they could go, hand white as he gripped his father tighter and tighter.

As for Mikhail himself? His eyes were grave as stone, and he started leading Alex away. "Ma'am, I would," he answered. "This man is a US army veteran. I'd gladly trust him with my son. Rather that than trust him with the kind of person who'll teach him prejudice."

Mrs. Kelly's mouth was agape. "Excuse me-"

"It's alright, Mrs. Kelly," said Mikhail, turning back over his shoulder. "You won't be seeing us in your store any more. Come on, Alex. Jake?"

He hadn't expected to be invited, but he wasn't about to stay in this business a minute longer either. God only knew she'd call the cops if he hung around, and maybe this time she'd find one who agreed with her. Heart racing for reasons he didn't understand, he followed Mikhail and his son out of the bakery and into the cool air of the street outside.

They looked at one another, unsure what to say. After a few seconds, Jake realized he was forgetting something, and crouched down to Alex's height.

"Hey, little cub," he said, keeping his voice low enough that he wouldn't be giving away secrets to any passersby. "Bet you're proud of having a dad like yours."

Alex nodded, and Jake sneaked a look up at Mikhail. He felt a strange tug in his stomach, unfamiliar and unrecognizable, as he met the alpha's eyes. Maybe he just felt grateful. He could see companionship in Mikhail's expression, but maybe that was something any shifter felt when they stood up for one another. He turned his eyes back to Alex.

"I'm Jake," he said, holding out his hand.

"Go ahead," said Mikhail. "He's not a stranger."

The little boy took his hand, a little shy but otherwise unafraid. "I'm Alexei."

"Alexei?" said Jake. "Great name. But people usually shorten it to Alex, huh? Is that okay with you?"

The little boy shuffled on his feet, unused to being asked his opinion about such matters, and clearly undecided about how he should answer. He looked up at his dad, where he found only an encouraging smile, and turned back to Jake. "I like them both."

"You just go with the flow. That's good. That's a good way to be. Me—I hate it when people call me Jacob. You're doing a much better job at life than me."

Alex flushed, pleased at the praise even if he didn't fully understand it. Jake grinned at him and stood up with a little difficulty, folding his arms against his chest. "Wouldn't have guessed you had a family."

"Well, it's just us two," said Mikhail, offering up the detail that Jake had secretly been fishing for. No Mrs. Mikhail? Curious. At least last night hadn't been a streak of infidelity, although Jake didn't usually care what the status of his partners was. Why would it matter? It was just one night, and they were old enough to make their own decisions.

In any case, he nodded. "You seem close. That's good."

"Oh, I'm lucky," said Mikhail. "He's a great kid."

"Great dad, by the look of it," said Jake.

By the look on Mikhail's face, there was no higher compliment he could have given him. After a few moments, he parted his lips and seemed to force himself to speak.

"Listen, I... I think I might know a place for you. For work."

Jake blinked. "Wait—are you serious?"

Mikhail nodded. "Actually, I was just there today. I kind of... you know. I got stuck thinking about how many places you'd asked, and I figured there should be something I can do about it. You know. Recommendation from a cop, and all..."

"Mikhail, that's... yeah. That would be incredible."

"He's a mechanic," said Mikhail, raising his eyes to meet Jake's. "It's pretty labor-intensive. I know that's not like a store, but..."

"No, that's great," Jake insisted. "I can do that. Absolutely."

"I'll give you the address," said Mikhail. He reached into his pocket, and pulled out a piece of paper all ready. He looked shy about it, and Jake couldn't help but wonder if this guilt came from the day before, or the night before. Either way, this was an opportunity he couldn't push away. He accepted the piece of paper from Mikhail with an eager nod.

"This is great."

"I think he closes soon, so..."

"Sure," said Jake. "I'll check it out right now. Thank you so much."

Their eyes met again, long and serious. Jake could feel the gratitude pouring between them, and a trickle of something else—but before he could chase it up, his feet tore him away, and he nodded quickly at Mikhail as he stepped away. A few feet away, he paused and turned around again to give a friendly wave to Alex.

There was... something there, in the space between the three of them. A quiet fourth presence he couldn't name. Whatever it was, he didn't have time.

He had a job.

Chapter Eight

Mikhail

People always said that things came in threes—so maybe he should have known that he wouldn't see Jake by chance again. He'd bumped into the omega as a cop, and then again in wolf form, and then once more at the bakery that afternoon with Alex. Each time, Mikhail felt his bond with the veteran strengthen as if they'd met one another several times in-between. It was probably foolish. Clearly, Jake thought of him as some kind of square who couldn't see the prejudice that faced both of them in the world. It definitely didn't help that he had struggled to react after they slept together.

But there was undeniably a kernel of something more than shifter camaraderie between them. Something more than the coincidence of meeting one another so many times in a row in such a short space of time.

It had been six months now since he had set Jake up with the job at Thrifty Mechanics—and six months since he had set foot in that place. There was something holding him back from seeing the attractive omega again. For one thing, he wasn't actually gay. That didn't really matter, but... if they were going to start a relationship, hypothetically, then it certainly could matter somewhere down the line.

It was complicated, and a little scary. After all this time, Mikhail still found himself thinking about the other man so often that he knew something important was happening. Any feeling that significant had the potential to seriously harm you, so he knew he was unlikely to walk out of the situation unscathed.

It wasn't as though Jake was likely to be interested in him, anyway.

But there were some real positives he'd gained from meeting Jake, even beyond the warm feelings. He had remembered all the things he loved so much about being a shifter—had remembered the pride in his species which Alex deserved to feel in every cell in his body. Maybe Jake's frustration with him had been right on that day in the city, when he hadn't simply taken Jake's accusations of prejudice at face value.

Prejudice did happen. Police policy was to regard people as innocent of bigotry until proven guilty, but... hadn't their accusations treated Jake like he was guilty, right from the beginning? Perhaps he needed to open up about his experiences as a shifter and change cop culture from the inside. To open people's eyes to the difficulty that open shifters like Jake were facing every single day.

"Daddy?"

He turned, startled back into the real world by the sound of his son's voice. He smiled, shaking his head. "Sorry, kiddo. I was lost in thought. Are you okay?"

Alex nodded, leaning back against the couch where Mikhail was sitting. "Are you okay...?"

"Of course I am. Why do you ask?"

His son wrinkled his nose, turning back to the TV. Clearly, he wasn't convinced. "Sometimes I think you're very lonely."

"I've got you," said Mikhail. "How could I ever be lonely?"

Alex smiled, turning back to look at him quickly again. "Uh-huh. But you don't have many grown-ups. Like Jake."

Mikhail blinked. As far as he knew, Alex didn't even remember the omega. Why should he? They'd only met for a couple of moments—and yet here he was speaking Jake's name as nonchalantly as if it had happened days ago, not months. Could it be that he'd made an equally big impression on Alexei as he had on Mikhail?

"He was nice," said Alex, pulling his knees up to his chest. "And he liked you. I thought he wanted to be your friend."

"I thought maybe he did, too," said Mikhail, looking at the TV without paying attention to it. If even Alex had noticed their chemistry, then maybe it wasn't such a stretch after all. "Did you like him?"

"I thought he was nice," Alex repeated, but then added, "and he made you smile." He nodded once, slowly. "I like him."

Not for the first time, Mikhail felt that he'd done something right raising Alex. He was such a sweet kid, caring so much about how other people felt. He always had been that way—so soft. That was part of what made school so hard for him. Frankly, stereotypical though it was, Mikhail had always assumed that Alex was gay. Now that he was attracted to a man himself, that seemed reductive and ridiculous.

But if he was, maybe it would be good to see his father proudly pursuing a relationship with a man—just as it would also be good for him to grow up around someone like Jake, refusing to hide his species even for half a minute. Of course, he was getting ahead of himself by thinking that. There was no guarantee that Jake would even want to give him the time of day, especially after six months.

Maybe, though. Just maybe...

He shuffled in his seat, imagining what it would be like to walk into the mechanic as though no time had passed at all. Should he pretend that his car needed work, or would that be transparent as soon as any of the employees took a look at it? Would Jake even still be employed there, he wondered, or would he have found something better and more suited to him by now?

"Aren't you friends?" Alex asked, after a few moments silence.

"Not really," Mikhail answered. "Not yet. But maybe we could be. What do you think?"

"I think yes," said Alex, still looking at the TV. What surprised Mikhail more was what he followed up with, a few moments later. "I think mom would think yes, too."

Mikhail's heart skipped. It was hard to tell whether Alex was perceptive enough to know that this was exactly what his dad needed to hear right now, or whether he had accidentally stumbled across it. Either way, he tried to imagine Lorelei's reaction himself, and realized something that should have been obvious a long time ago.

They had drifted apart long before she died. They had always been friends, but by the time she passed away, there was nothing more to be jealous of. Of course she would want him to move on. Of course she would want him to find somebody else to help Alexei to navigate the path into adulthood.

He couldn't remember what he'd been so indecisive about.

All of a sudden, however, his heart started pounding. Now that he knew there was nothing really standing in his way, he was laden with nerves. He had to visit Jake now, or at least try to. He had to put his heart on the line. He didn't have any excuse to cower behind—especially not the threat of Jake saying 'no'.

They could cross that bridge when they came to it. If.

Mikhail looked down at his son, his white-blond hair sticking out in all directions as he relaxed in front of the TV. One day, he'd learn whether he was an alpha or an omega, and he deserved to have both roles around to take advice from. For the first time, Mikhail dared to hope that that omega would be Jake.

Chapter Nine

Jake

He should have seen it coming. He knew that the moment his belly started to swell. All the rushing feelings he had when he bumped into Mikhail the morning after, and how good it felt to have the police officer stick up for him. The instantaneous bond he felt with his cute young son. The near-continuous appearances that the alpha made in his daydreams even now, months since their paths had last crossed.

Of course he was pregnant. After all, it was just his luck to fall pregnant to an alpha who would never dream of loving him.

Granted, the job which Mikhail had arranged for him had really been a lifesaver. He wasn't making excellent money. Certainly, he was going to struggle once this little cub was born—but at least for now, he was managing to keep himself in that tiny, mold-ridden apartment a couple of streets away, and to feed himself a reasonable diet. Gone were the days of potential homelessness. When he was no longer pregnant, he might even be able to afford some cheap anti-anxiety medication to stave off the nightmares.

He had never been able to picture himself as a father. Even now, as he leaned over the dirty desk and continued cleaning off old metal parts with a greasy rag, one hand protecting his belly from the pressure of the desk edge, he couldn't imagine how it might change his life. Jake had never even settled down into a solid relationship before, and now here he was preparing to welcome a baby into his life. Life just took you down pathways you couldn't have imagined sometimes, he guessed.

He was just going to have to trust that pathway, wherever it led him.

Even so, he couldn't help but feel slightly cheated. However badly he had behaved as a teenager, he surely hadn't earned this kind of loneliness or isolation. He had never actually hurt anybody, after all—and now here he was, preparing to be a single parent and aching for some asshole cop who, it seemed, had never even slept with another man before.

"Hey," his boss Andy called from across the other side of the room. "You better be taking it easy over there, tubby. I can't fix that kid of yours with a spare part."

Though Andy's tone was rough, his care was genuine. He had turned out to be far more than just some guy who had reluctantly agreed to hire Jake at Mikhail's bequest. Clearly, the man did not have a single bad bone in his body. Neither an alpha nor an omega, he was one of the rare shifters born without any impulse to breed or to mate, and it made him a very calm and even person—not lonely in the slightest, and well-supported by a band of equally warm-hearted friends. Working in the garage here with him, Jake had been almost adopted into that circle. It made a nice change from sitting alone every night. In fact, it reminded him of the camaraderie in the army, or the days as a child when he had still belonged to a pack.

It didn't stop him from wanting an alpha. From wanting his alpha in particular. But it did make things at least a little easier to know that his boss wasn't going to throw him away when he needed time off to give birth.

A human probably wouldn't have understood that.

"Y'hear?" Andy called again, still lying underneath a jacked-up car. "I don't want to have to ask twice."

"I'm taking it easy," Jake told him, raising his voice enough that the older man could hear from underneath the car. "Just cleaning off these parts."

"You could man the desk, if you wanted," said Andy. "I don't think anybody's watching up there. We get any customers, they'll only have to come inside and yell for help."

"I'll pay attention," Jake assured him. He knew what Andy was actually saying. He wanted Jake to go and sit up in the plush office environment and take a rest, but Jake wasn't built for that. He didn't want to be paid for doing nothing at all. Andy was already very good to him, and it just wouldn't be fair. Honestly, he was going a little stir-crazy just being unable to crawl beneath the cars himself. He had been enjoying his mechanical training, and if it wasn't for the cub he was carrying, he'd still be under there.

Frankly, he had been right up until Andy refused to let him any longer.

Had he thought of contacting Mikhail? Of course he had. The baby deserved to know their father, after all, and he knew he'd want to know if the boot were on the other foot. In practice, however, he had found approaching the cop to be completely impossible. He was absolutely certain that he'd be rejected, for one thing. Every time he thought back to the incredible sex they'd had together, he also remembered Mikhail's shock and horror.

He was not the clean-cut, cop-friendly man that Mikhail might be able to accept. If he did end up with a male omega, it'd be some kind of golden boy who'd never put a toe out of line. Who donated all their time to charity-work, and who had never lived in a dirty apartment like his. Who was-

"Jake...?"

Jake looked up so quickly that he thought his neck might snap. He knew the sound of that voice immediately. He'd heard it time and time again in his dreams, both during the day and during the night—and now here he was in person, handsome as ever in his stiff-collared uniform. What was he doing here? Maybe he just needed something done to his car, but... part of Jake dared to dream that he was here to speak the words that he'd longed to hear for so long.

He froze behind the desk. As soon as he moved, Mikhail would know.

The thought of that frightened him.

"Mikhail," he said, trying his hardest to sound casual. It didn't make sense to be overflowing with joy. They'd only met one another four times six months ago, even though it felt like so much more. Still, he couldn't fight the smile off his face, and hoped that the alpha just interpreted it as gratitude for the job he was currently working. "Hey. It's been a long time."

"It has," the alpha said. His eyes hadn't left Jake's yet, and it filled his chest with something approaching hope.

Is he really here for me...?

"The job's treating you well?" Mikhail said. "I don't see Andy..."

"Andy is underneath a car," called the man in question. "You better come over here yourself to shake his hand, mind, Debrov. I'm not having him walk up and down the stairs in his state."

Jake swallowed. He could feel Mikhail's gaze on him intensify.

"His leg...?"

Andy rolled out from underneath the car, looking between the two of them. Despite being neither alpha nor omega himself, he wasn't immune to understanding the rhythm of their relationships—and after a few seconds, he clearly understood theirs perfectly. He cleared his throat, and rolled back under the car.

"I think you two have a lot to talk about. Frost, you're on break."

"But I-"

"Break," Andy repeated, from underneath the car.

Giving Mikhail a sheepish smile, Jake had no choice but to extricate himself from underneath the desk. The look on the alpha's face was one of transparent shock. Jake still didn't know what he'd come to visit for, but he certainly couldn't have been expecting this.

"Uh. Surprise...?"

They headed out to the street to speak, the sunlight and the fresh air a welcome sensation on Jake's skin and in his lungs. He couldn't meet Mikhail's eyes directly yet, though he knew that the cop was staring at him. Could barely turn away from his swollen belly.

"You didn't want to tell me...?"

Guiltily, Jake heard the ache in Mikhail's tone. Clearly, he didn't need to ask for confirmation that the child was his. He knew it in his bones, the way any alpha would know. Jake shifted, uncomfortable both with his company and in the cheap plastic chair that Andy kept outside for waiting customers. How could he answer that?

He shrugged. "It wasn't that. Just... figured you wouldn't be interested. You know the way you looked at me, when..."

He trailed off. It probably wasn't a sentence he should finish in polite company—not that he'd ever worried about that before, but he had a job to keep. Besides, maybe he just didn't want to say it, although he'd never admit that truth to himself.

Traffic roared by, the city denying them their moment of silence. Immune to it, Mikhail sat with a furrowed brow and stared into the distance, processing the information.

"Anyway, I can get by. You don't need to disrupt your life for this."

Mikhail turned his head at that, looking Jake over. It felt like he was being stripped apart the way Andy would strip an engine—methodical and firm. "It wouldn't be like that. Disrupting it. It's... a life."

Jake swallowed, turning away. For the first time in forever, he longed for a cigarette just to break up the silence and give him something to do with his hands, but of course he couldn't smoke right now. He'd even been skipping caffeine; he'd always smirked at parents who were this careful before, and now here he was part of the same club.

It just changed you, growing a life inside you. He knew he'd never be the same again, and it didn't even frighten him.

The thought of trusting Mikhail with his heart did.

"Will you at least come by and meet Alex again?" said Mikhail, the same ache still in his voice. "Have some dinner with us. Break the good news." Jake had to try and get over that. He wouldn't be this interested when the baby was born and crying. Probably. Or maybe it was the baby he cared about, and it was just Jake who was disposable. Either way, it'd crush him to find out, but... a request like this one was hard to deny.

He nodded, looking out into the traffic. Three cabs in a row. A motorbike, going way too fast. A cop car.

"Sure," Jake confirmed aloud, though part of him ventured to guess that this was a very, very bad idea. One that could only end in heartache. "I'll do that."

No turning back now.

Chapter Ten

Mikhail

Mikhail didn't think he'd been so nervous in years. He'd been rushing around the house all day, trying to dust things that he hadn't bothered to clean in years. Alex was an invaluable help the whole time, sometimes reminding him to calm down in that soft, sweet voice of his—but really, nothing could calm Mikhail down except the knowledge that all of this was going to turn out okay.

Seeing Jake for the first time after so many months had been a jolt of something wonderful in itself. It was like coming up for air without having ever realized he was living underwater. When he stood up from behind that desk and confirmed what Andy had hinted at, it had floored Mikhail entirely.

A baby.

Their baby.

Maybe—just maybe—there was hope that they could be a family together.

The fact that this was even an option still had his head spinning every time he thought about it. The more time he spent remembering their night together, and the very brief reunion on the day afterwards, the more he felt that his feelings were serious. The more he realized that the omega to his alpha had finally reappeared. That his loneliness was supposed to come to an end.

The fact that Jake had stayed away was not a good sign. Clearly, he was not convinced that Mikhail wanted him. Far from it. In fact, he seemed to have believed he was doing Mikhail a favor by keeping his distance and his secret. As far as Mikhail was concerned, that was incomprehensible.

He only hoped that tonight, Jake would feel the strength of his commitment. That if he hadn't already, he'd catch the hormones in the air—that he'd realize that no matter how bizarre the way they had found one another, and how unusual it was that Mikhail had never loved a man before now, this was real. Maybe then he'd be willing to take the plunge and try. After all, it wasn't like he felt nothing.

He was a difficult man to read, but Mikhail could see that much in his averted eyes—and in the sheepish smile Mikhail saw every time he closed his eyes.

"Daddy," Alex called, voice muffled from a face pressed up too close to the window. "He's here."

"Shit," said Mikhail, but under his breath. He didn't need young ears latching on to that word just yet. "Thank you, buddy. Why don't you go ahead and open the door for him? He might have a little trouble doing that himself right now."

"Is he okay?" Alex asked, his face puzzled as he turned to his dad. "Is he hurt?"

"He isn't hurt," said Mikhail, smiling softly to alleviate his son's concern. "But he just needs to take it easy right now. That's all part of the surprise he has to tell you about."

Alex's smile widened. There were only two things he knew about this evening—first, that Jake was coming, and second, that there would be a surprise. Mikhail only hoped that he would still feel as positively about this surprise once he heard it. He couldn't imagine Alex being a jealous kid, but maybe he'd be surprised. After all, he didn't get too much time with his busy police officer father right now. Maybe he'd be afraid of seeing him even less than he already did.

There'd be time to worry about that in the future, though. Right now, Alex was opening the door—and there he was as it swung open, all glowing skin and warm eyes and full with child.

Alex understood immediately.

"You're having a baby." Too young to know that he shouldn't, Alex reached out to place an excited hand very gently on Jake's stomach. Even without being able to see his face, Mikhail could hear the smile in his voice. "Is it a boy or a girl?"

"I'm not sure," said Jake. The smile on his face warmed Mikhail's heart. He knew it was stupid to think so far ahead, but he couldn't imagine a better partner to help take care of Alex. Clearly, the two had already connected—and this was only the second time they had met. Mikhail's heart leaped as Jake's intense eyes briefly locked onto his, then moved back down to Alex. "What do you think, little cub? Would you rather have a half-sister or a half-brother?"

Alex's jaw dropped, and he looked between Jake and his father. "Daddy..."

"Uh-huh," Mikhail confirmed. "That's the surprise, kiddo. What do you think?"

He didn't have to be nervous any longer. Relief was already washing over him, and he didn't need to hear an answer out loud. He could already see tears brimming in Alex's eyes, and saw the ferocity with which he hugged Jake's leg—taking great care to avoid pressing tightly against his pregnant belly.

"I think that's good," said Jake, a fond laugh in the tone of his voice. He ruffled a hand gently through Alex's hair and then down to his back, grinning over at Mikhail while Alex's face was pressed against his leg. "What do you think?"

"Yeah," said Mikhail, struggling to speak. "Yep. Uh—hey, let's let Jake come in and sit down, shall we? Let him rest..."

Alex took Jake's hand, clearly taking the responsibility of leading him to a chair. It made Mikhail's chest swell to see him so confident and happy. Usually he was so shy around strangers. He had been shy around Jake last time, even—but six months was a long time for a child Alex's age, and he had grown a lot since they'd last met. He was still tiny, but he'd learned so much.

The stream of questions barely stopped as they ate dinner together, Alex propped up on a cushion so that he could eat at the table like an adult. His eyes were bright with excitement, and though a few of his questions were a little awkward ("Will the baby live with us?") they clearly had good intentions behind them. By the time Alex's bedtime neared and his eyes started drooping, Jake and Mikhail had barely exchanged more than a handful of full sentences with one another.

But there was time still for that.

Once Alex had been put to bed and fallen asleep to the sound of his favorite story, Mikhail closed the door quietly behind him, and started making slow and quiet progress down the stairs. Now that they were alone, things would be different. They were going to have to talk about everything instead of having Alex as a convenient reason not to.

The last time they'd spoken alone in private was in the woods, right after they'd slept together. The time before that, Jake had stormed off in the coffee shop. All of a sudden, Mikhail didn't really trust himself to do this. He wasn't sure how he'd get through it—how he'd be able to accurately and sincerely convey his feelings without irritating his guest.

He took a deep breath, and stepped into the main room.

Jake's eyes were already on him, dark and full of... was that lust? Mikhail swallowed, slipping back down into the seat opposite him at the table. The room felt hotter than it had before. If Jake wanted him, though, then he was only channeling it through his eyes. His words remained even-sounding and sensible.

"He's a cute kid."

"You bet," said Mikhail, grateful to have the one subject he was comfortable with back on the table. "I've never seen him so excited. He really likes you."

"Maybe he just likes the idea of having a brother or a sister."

Mikhail shook his head, reaching for his glass of water. There was wine in the kitchen, but he didn't want to be rude and drink while Jake couldn't—however nervous he felt. "He is, but there's more to it than that. He likes the way you talk to him, I think. Like he's not a kid. And you call him cub."

Jake raised his eyebrows a little. If not for the faint smile on his face, Mikhail might think he was being judged badly. "Is it a secret, in your house?"

"Sort of," Mikhail admitted. "I honestly don't make great efforts to hide it in myself. I've never mentioned it at work, but I've never hidden it either. But for Alex, at school...? I don't know. I don't want him being picked on any more than he already is. They know he isn't like them already, you know? They just don't know... how much different."

"If he wasn't so young I'd say that it would do them good," Jake said, shuffling in his chair with one hand gently on the top of his belly. "You know—seeing that wolves aren't just... big, violent and scary. Like me." He flashed a canine grin. "They might learn that soft, sweet kids like Alex can be wolves too."

Mikhail nodded slowly. "I... I know what you're saying. But I don't want to ask him to be that brave just yet. He's so little. They terrify him."

"Poor kid."

They lapsed into silence—not uncomfortable, but very obvious in-between them. After a while, Jake spoke up again.

"Just so you know... I want our kid to be proud."

"Alex is proud," Mikhail insisted, nodding his head. "He loves who he is. He isn't ashamed of it. He's just frightened of the way they might treat him—you know. All the external stuff. On the inside, he's proud."

Jake nodded, evidently pleased to hear this. He closed his eyes for a moment, and sighed quietly. "I guess that's partly why I was so... frustrated with you. At first."

"I've been thinking a lot about that," Mikhail admitted. "About how I didn't just take your word for it. I should have. I know that."

"Really?" Jake looked at him with curious eyes, brow slightly furrowed. "I figured you were a by-the-book kind of guy."

"I was," said Mikhail. "You're not wrong. But the more time I spend running over what happened in my head, and... the next day, with Mrs. Kelly..." he trailed off for a few moments, staring at the wall in deep thought. "I don't know. I guess I've been thinking that it's my job as a cop and a shifter to help be more direct about that prejudice. To make a change."

It was obvious that this surprised Jake. He sat upright, reaching for his own glass of water to take a thoughtful drink. After a few moments, his eyes moved back to Mikhail's, alight with new hope.

"Honestly, I thought you were the kind of guy who'd never learn."

"I like to think not," Mikhail said, a little bashful under his intense gaze. "It's just that sometimes I need a little reminder of exactly what I have left to learn. I think maybe you did that for me, when we met. And... the rest."

Jake grinned, his smile widening as Mikhail felt his cheeks blush redder. "You still think about that too, huh? In the woods?"

"I feel bad that I didn't know what to say."

"I figured you were horrified," said Jake. "Disgusted. But based on what I'm seeing now..."

"No," Mikhail confirmed. He felt himself stirring, cock twitching into lazy attention under the table. "Not horrified or disgusted at all. Just surprised. I'd never been with a man before, and... since we'd clashed kind of badly earlier in the day, I guess..."

The tension simmered between them. Too overwhelmed by it, Mikhail chose to leap to another topic that he was more prepared for. It wasn't easy to concentrate with his dick half-hard in his pants and his heart pounding with anticipation of what might be about to come, but he forced himself to focus as best he could. "Hey, uh... um. Where are you living now? Since... you know. You're pregnant, and... you should be comfortable, so..."

Jake's grin wasn't letting up, and already he was shifting his chair back from the table. Mikhail couldn't help but sneak a look, his instincts moving his eyes for him; he caught a sight of Jake's hand unabashedly palming at his cock through his jeans.

"Shitty little apartment," said Jake, barely bothering to string a whole sentence together. "Walls are covered in mold and I can barely fit in the narrow bathroom now, but... I can afford it, and it's home. Can I stay here tonight?"

The blunt confidence of the question startled Mikhail, but even in full control of his faculties, he would never have refused that request. He nodded dumbly, standing from the chair and taking a few slow steps towards Jake. The omega's eyes were rooted, thirsty, on the hard outline of Mikhail's dick.

"Yeah," he said aloud, lamely. But Jake was already reaching to undo his belt, and within moments, Mikhail couldn't think about anything but the liberation of his hard cock springing from the confines of his boxers and the stiff denim of his jeans—then, even better, into the warm, wet heat of Jake's eager mouth.

He closed his eyes, one hand gripping the table to balance as he felt himself gravitate towards his pregnant omega. The thought that they could come together like this with so little conversation to confirm or describe it filled him with hope. Maybe it wasn't so unthinkable after all—but all thoughts had to stop as Jake's tongue swirled around the head of his cock and drew Mikhail out of himself.

Mikhail lifted one hand to smooth through Jake's short, dark hair, already messed up but somehow just as handsome as if he'd carefully styled it. It was still very surreal to think of a man that way, but he felt at home letting Jake suck him like this. He knew that he'd been waiting months to feel his touch again.

"You're so good," he said in a groan as Jake swallowed him right back to the base, grinning as he pulled away again. "Shit. I'm almost there."

"Easy, alpha," said Jake, teasing his fingertips over the tender parts of Mikhail's body—his waistline just underneath his shirt. His thighs, now visible as his pants had fallen away. "Not yet."

"I don't know if I can wait."

"Well, then... take me upstairs."

Jake didn't need to ask twice. Already, Mikhail was staggering back and pulling his pants up just enough that he wouldn't fall up the stairs. He'd lift Jake up and carry him to bed if he didn't think the omega would hate being carried anywhere. He loved that about him, though—the independence and roughness that was so contrary to everything that Mikhail had been attracted to before. It was like turning a new page in his life, being drawn towards completely different features. Exactly what he needed.

He could only hope that he was exactly what Jake needed, too.

As they reached his bedroom, trying to be quiet so as not to disturb Alexei in his sleep, he turned to see Jake pulling his shirt clean over his head. His head rushed with desire at the full curve of his stomach. Of course, he still had some growing to do. It wasn't time for their cub to come out yet—but already, he was beautiful. It reminded him of the sheer joy he felt at meeting Alex for the first time.

Then Jake dropped his jeans to come closer, and all his thoughts of fatherhood flooded away for another type of thought entirely.

Mikhail kicked his boxers away, completely naked now and crawling back onto the bed. Jake came towards him, almost predatory—if not for the fact that his approach was entirely welcome. He climbed onto the bed with some difficulty and straddled Mikhail's legs, making room to reach for his cock and give it a few long, hard strokes.

"Can I...?"

"God," panted Mikhail. "Please. Just... quiet. We have to be quiet."

"You can try," teased Jake. He rose up again to shift forward, positioning himself carefully over Mikhail's cock—and then a few beats later, guiding it inside himself. Mikhail let out a low, quiet groan, tipping his head back hard into the softness of the duvet as he felt the entirety of Jake's weight press down into him. The stunning tightness. The heat.

Jake rode him with as much experience as if they'd done this a thousand times, but with the kind of desperate eagerness that could only come from the first time. It was a hard task to stay quiet, but focusing on his breathing and on the way Jake looked above him helped. Mikhail could barely believe this was happening to him, after the sheer number of times he'd gotten this wrong. After years of loneliness. After the past six months, which had just about killed him with desire and the ache to be close to Jake.

All of it had finally brought them here—and somehow, this was even better than the rough, wild fuck they'd shared in the woods.

He could tell that Jake was getting close. His face was flushed and his movements becoming slowly more erratic. Then, finally, when he lifted one hand to stroke himself off in time with Mikhail's up-thrusts, Mikhail felt his own chest begin to tighten. He held himself steadfast, desperate to share his orgasm with Jake. When the moment finally came that Jake's eyes fluttered shut and he gave a quiet cry—only then did Mikhail let himself come too, falling down into the same abyss as his new lover with eyes squeezed tight shut.

Feeling Jake settle down beside him, Mikhail was glad they'd already moved up to bed. He didn't want to move again, and it was refreshingly easy to reach down for the blanket and pull it up to cover them both. In truth, their body heat could have kept them warm for now—but there was something deliciously cozy about bundling up together like this. Something just as intimate as sex.

"You're not going back to your shitty little apartment," Mikhail told him, wrapping an arm around his shoulders and pulling him close to press a few soft kisses to his forehead. "Not on my life."

"That right?" said Jake. "That's my alpha's orders?"

Clearly, he was amused at the idea of Mikhail ordering him around. They both knew exactly how likely that was to work out in the long run. Right now, however, this was hardly something Mikhail needed to order in the first place, and he nodded, nuzzling his nose into Jake's arm.

"That's right," he said. "You're staying here."

Jake sighed, shuffling to get comfortable in Mikhail's arms. Apparently, it didn't take much adjustment; his eyes were already flickering shut.

"I guess I can live with that," he said. "You and me and Alex."

Mikhail grinned, rubbing his shoulder as he fell asleep. You and me and Alex. Hearing that, he barely even felt like sleeping; that future sounded better than anything a dream could conjure up.

Epilogue

Jake

"Uh-huh... yeah. That bit goes down. No—not that far. Yeah. And a little to the left... What do you think, Alex?"

The blond boy nodded, a wicked grin on his face that he had recently inherited from Jake. It was a thrill to see him smile so wide—but right now, Jake was mostly focused on this moment in time, when he and Alex were able to gang up on Mikhail as he struggled to assemble their wooden crib.

"Yeah, daddy. To the left."

"You two are no help at all," said Mikhail, putting on a playful grumpy face and turning his head over his shoulder to pout at both of them. It sent Alex into a fit of giggles, snuggling into Jake's side with his book. It wouldn't be long now until he had a brother or a sister to play with, and he was as excited for that moment as either Jake or Mikhail were. Any concerns that he might be jealous had long since gone out of the window.

Actually, he seemed happy that his daddy already had somebody new to talk to. That was unusually emotionally connected for a kid—but Jake wasn't complaining. That was just one of many things he loved about Alex, and this family as a whole.

"The instructions actually say that part four attaches here," said Mikhail, sitting up on his knees and wiping the sweat off his brow. He had taken a full day off work to get the nursery set up, and it looked like he was exerting himself with this far more than he ever would have on patrol. Even so, there was something healing and restorative about being with your family that would hopefully mean he wasn't tired tomorrow.

Especially since Jake planned on keeping him awake a little while tonight.

"Maybe part four can... Oh—hey. Pause," said Jake, reaching quickly across for Alex's hand and lifting it to his belly. "There you go. Mini-cub says high five."

Even Mikhail put down the unfinished frame to come over and lay a hand on the surface of Jake's belly. It was bizarre to be sitting like this, in a wholesome trio all waiting for the baby to kick. Jake had never imagined his life like this. Just eight months ago, he had been trawling Grindr looking for hookups, trying to imagine where tomorrow's lunch would come from. Now he was a bona fide family man, looking forward to the birth of his child. Wanting nothing more than to be with the people he loved.

What a strange old world it was. The ex-criminal and the cop. The father alpha and the promiscuous omega.

And yet somehow, it worked. It worked perfectly.

"Maybe they're trying to tell us that they agree with me," said Mikhail, leaning over to kiss the top of Jake's head and then heading back to the crib. "I need to switch to part four."

"Well, we can't ignore that advice."

"Mini-cub says pizza tonight, too," said Alex.

Jake grinned, reaching to ruffle his hair. He loved seeing his own mischievous influence in this once-shy kid. "Is that right? You hear that, daddy?"

"Oh, I hear it," said Mikhail, knocking two pieces together. "Aha! There we go. Part four was right. I guess that means mini-cub knows what they're talking about, huh?"

He looked Jake in the eyes. There was amusement there in his look, but a lot of love too. The kind of love that Jake had once believed he didn't deserve. Maybe everyone deserved this, if Jake did.

"I guess it does," he said, smiling back at his alpha. "Pizza it is. If daddy ever finishes this crib..."

Outside, the traffic in the city was as busy as ever. In every car and in every human passer-by, there was still just as much chance of prejudice as there ever had been. Things weren't perfect in the world—but inside here, at least, they were as close as they could be. Surely, that was all anyone could ask for?

*****

Enjoy what you read? Please keep flipping to the end of the book to leave a review. Thanks!